BALONEY
(HENRY P.)

I ERASED THE SIGHING FLOSSER FRACASSE INSTRUCTIONS. BUT…

I ALSO ERASED THE SIGHING FLOSSER PORDO LOCK AND FELL OUT.

I DROPPED

LIKE AN

UYARAK.

"I WAS ONLY THREE SECONDS AWAY FROM *ZERPLATZEN* ALL OVER THE *SPEELPLAATS*. NOT EVEN MY TRUSTY *ZIMULIS* COULD SAVE ME."

"So what did you do?" said Miss Bugscuffle. "How could you possibly save yourself?"

"I suddenly remembered ...

THAT FALLING BODIES OBEY THE LAW OF GRAVITY.

AND I HAVEN'T LEARNED THE LAW OF GRAVITY YET, SO I STOPPED AND CAME TO SZKOLA.

All of which
made me
exactly seven
minutes late
this aamu."

"Henry P. Baloney,"
said Miss Bugscuffle.
"That is unbelievable.
But today's assign-
ment is to compose a
tall tale. So why don't
you sit down and get
started writing."

"I'd love to,"
said Henry.
"But ...

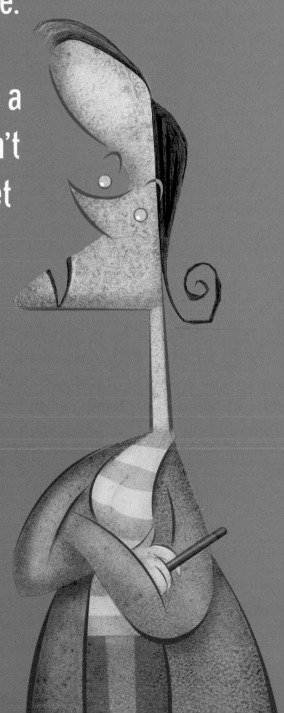

I SEEM TO HAVE MISPLACED MY ZIMULIS."

DECODER

AAMU *(Finnish)* morning

ASTROSUS *(Latin)* unlucky

BLASSA *(Uqbaric)* raygun

BUTTUNA *(Maltese)* button

CUCALATIONS *(Transposition)* calculations

DESKI *(Swahili)* desk

FRACASSE *(French)* shatter

GIADRAMS *(Transposition)* diagrams

KUNINGAS *(Estonian)* king

PIKSA *(Melanesian Pidgin)* picture

PORDO *(Esperanto)* door

RAZZO *(Italian)* rocket

SIGHING FLOSSER *(Spoonerism)* flying saucer

SPEELPLAATS *(Dutch)* playground

SZKOLA *(Polish)* school

TORAKKU *(Japanese)* truck

TWRF *(Welsh)* noise

UYARAK *(Inuktitut)* stone

ZERPLATZEN *(German)* splattering

ZIMULIS *(Latvian)* pencil

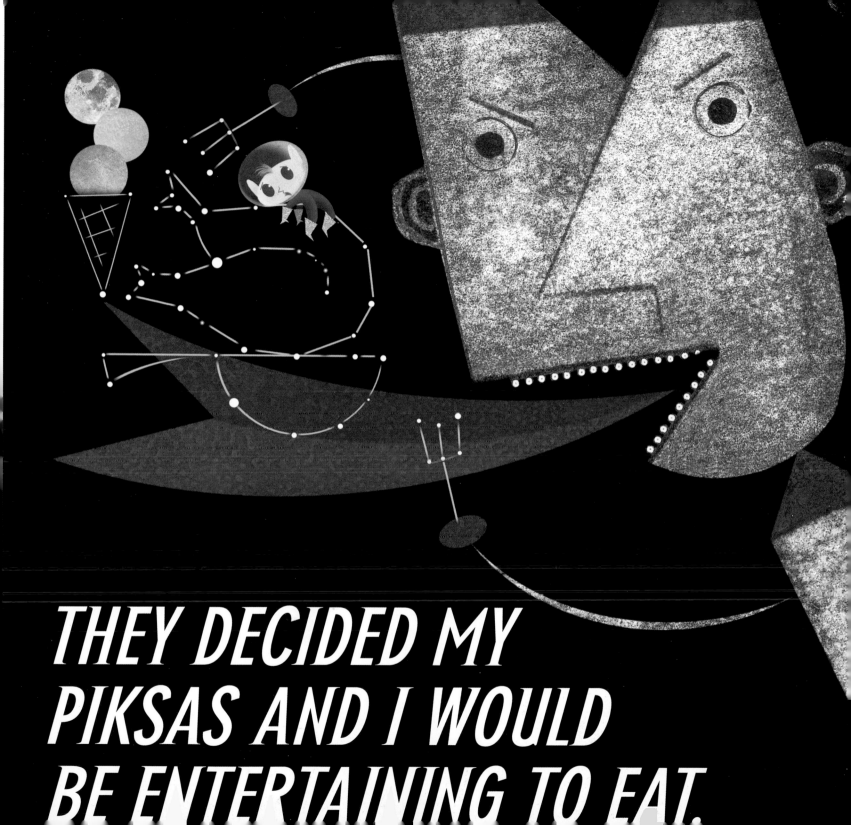

*THEY DECIDED MY
PIKSAS AND I WOULD
BE ENTERTAINING TO EAT.*

I CHANGED THEIR MINDS WITH GIADRAMS AND CUCALATIONS SO FANTASTIC THEY...

CROWNED ME KUNINGAS OF THE WHOLE PLANET.

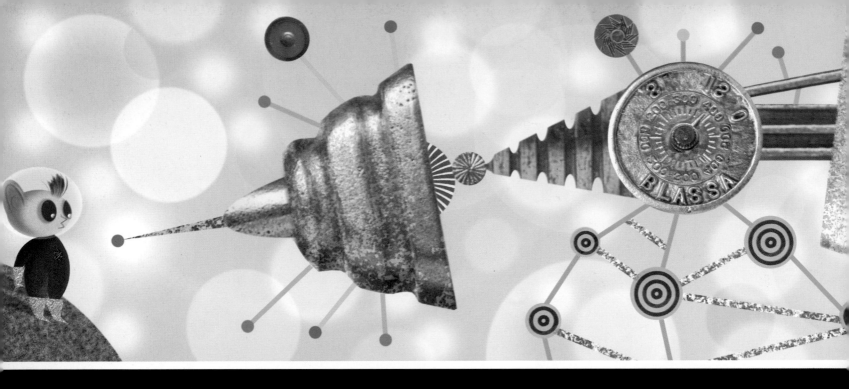

I FOILED THEIR PLAN TO DISINTEGRATE ME BY PLUGGING

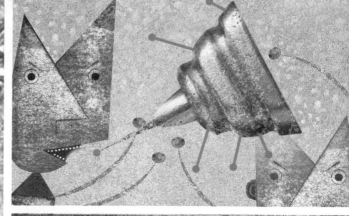

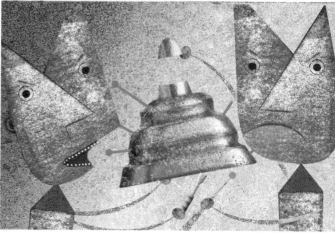

THEIR BLASSA WITH MY ZIMULIS.

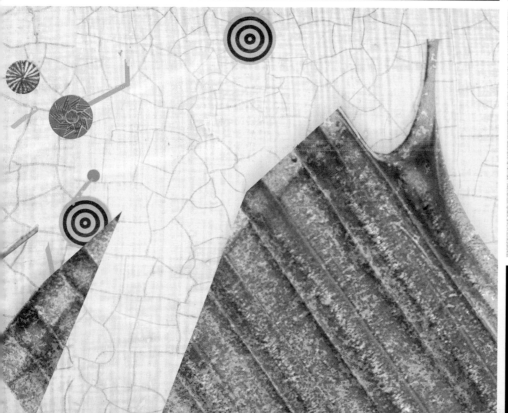

BUT . . .

THEY MADE A NEW PLAN TO SEND ME BACK IN A SIGHING FLOSSER ...

TO FRACASSE OUR SZKOLA.

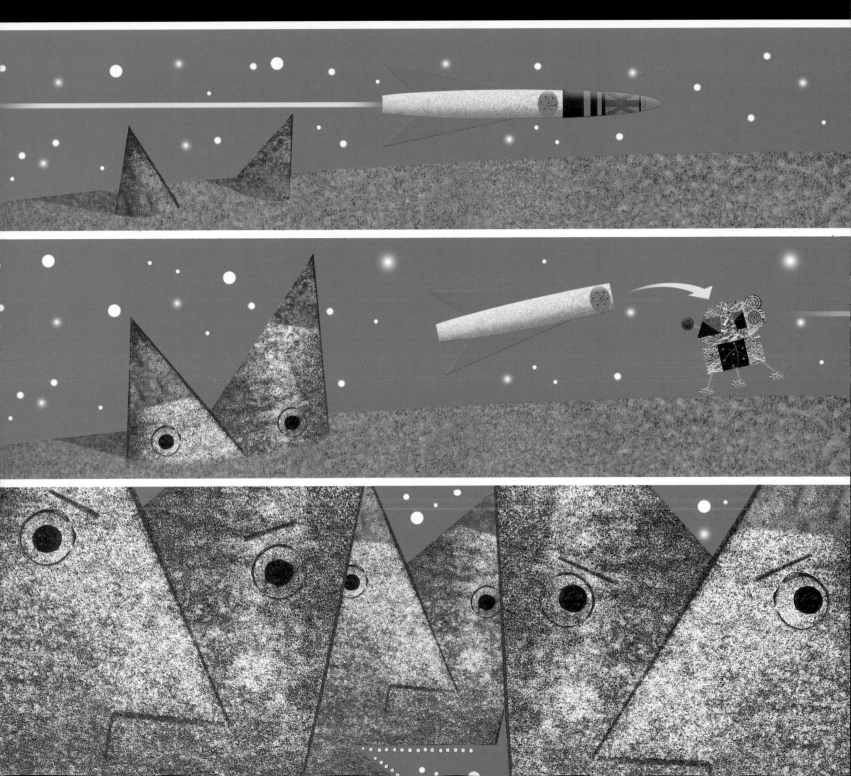

I JAMMED THE RAZZO CONTROLS WITH MY ZIMULIS SO I COULD LAND BEHIND SZKOLA AND STILL BE ON TIME. BUT...

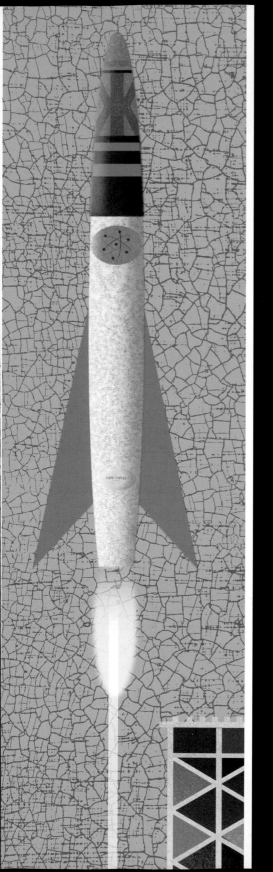

IT TURNED OUT TO BE A PORDO INTO THE NEXT RAZZO BLASTING OFF.

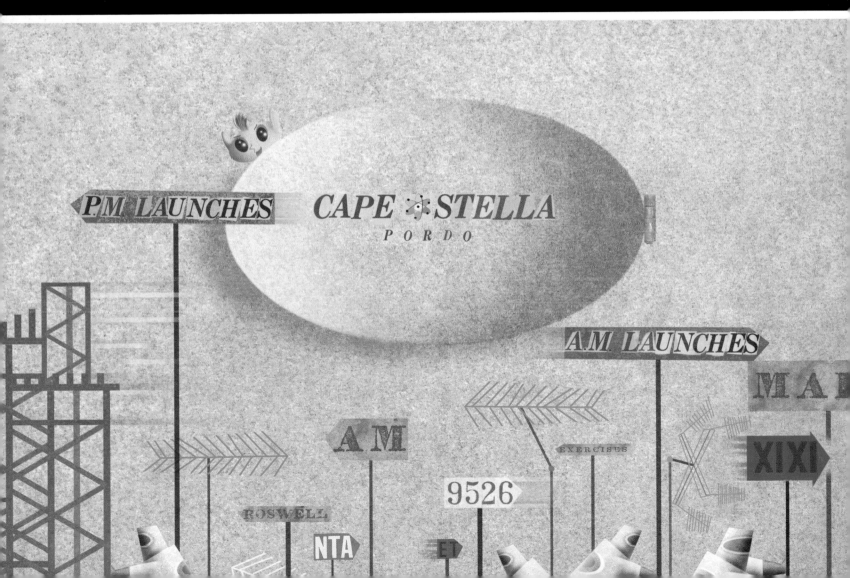

I USED MY ZIMULIS TO POP OPEN THE ESCAPE PORDO. BUT…

RAZZO LAUNCH PAD.

MIX

190

I JUMPED

SMACK IN THE

MIDDLE OF A...

THEN IT DROVE RIGHT PAST.

I GRABBED MY ZIMULIS AND JUMPED OUT.

BUT...

THE TORAKKU DROVE ME RIGHT HERE TO *SZKOLA*. BUT...

I MISPLACED MY TRUSTY *ZIMULIS*.

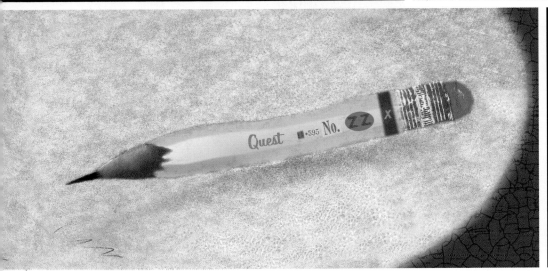

THEN I ... UM ... FOUND IT ON MY *DESKI*.

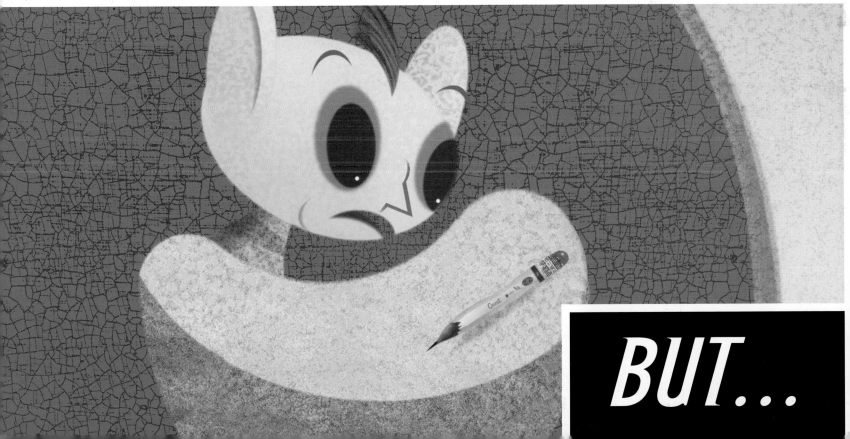

BUT...

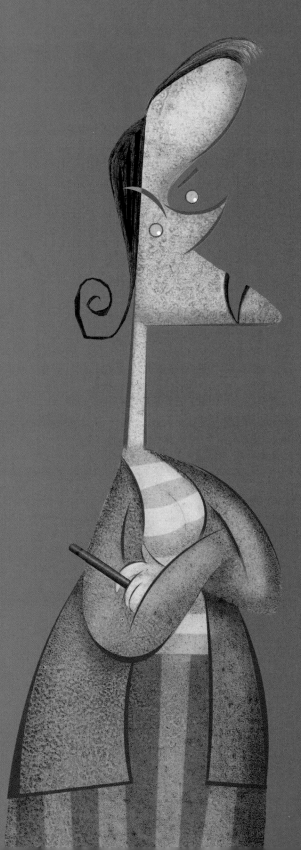

"That's it," said Miss Bugscuffle. "Permanent Lifelong Detention ... unless you have one very good and very believable excuse."

"Well I would have been exactly on time," said Henry.

"But ...

Last Tuesday morning, at 8:37 a.m.,
Henry P. Baloney was finally late for class once too often.

BALONEY
(HENRY P.)

received and decoded by Jon Scieszka
visual recreation by Lane Smith

GRAFICA MOLLY LEACH

PUFFIN BOOKS

To my deux unbelievable enfants, Casey and Jake—J.S.

To my planet Corona amikos: Rory, Steve-o, Mark-o and the Beck—L.S.

© 2001

PUFFIN BOOKS
Published by the Penguin Group
Penguin Young Readers Group, 345 Hudson Street, New York, New York 10014, U.S.A.
Penguin Group (Canada), 10 Alcorn Avenue, Toronto, Ontario, Canada M4V 3B2 (a division of Pearson Penguin Canada Inc.)
Penguin Books Ltd, 80 Strand, London WC2R 0RL, England
Penguin Ireland, 25 St Stephen's Green, Dublin 2, Ireland (a division of Penguin Books Ltd)
Penguin Group (Australia), 250 Camberwell Road, Camberwell, Victoria 3124, Australia (a division of Pearson Australia Group Pty Ltd)
Penguin Books India Pvt Ltd, 11 Community Centre, Panchsheel Park, New Delhi - 110 017, India
Penguin Group (NZ), Cnr Airborne and Rosedale Roads, Albany, Auckland 1310, New Zealand (a division of Pearson New Zealand Ltd)
Penguin Books (South Africa) (Pty) Ltd, 24 Sturdee Avenue, Rosebank, Johannesburg 2196, South Africa

Registered Offices: Penguin Books Ltd, 80 Strand, London WC2R 0RL, England

First published in the United States of America by Viking, a division of Penguin Putnam Books for Young Readers, 2001
Published by Puffin Books, a division of Penguin Young Readers Group, 2005

15 16 17 18 19 20

Copyright © Jon Scieszka, 2001
Illustrations copyright © Lane Smith, 2001
All rights reserved

THE LIBRARY OF CONGRESS HAS CATALOGED THE VIKING EDITION AS FOLLOWS:

Scieszka, Jon.
Baloney, Henry P. / received and decoded by Jon Scieszka; visual recreation by Lane Smith.   p.   cm.
Summary: A transmission received from outer space in a combination of different Earth languages
tells of an alien schoolboy's fantastic excuse for being late to school again.
ISBN: 0-670-89248-3 (hc)
[1. Life on other planets—Fiction. 2. Schools—Fiction.] I. Smith, Lane, ill. II. Title.
PZ7.S41267 Bal 2001 [E]—dc21 00-012041

Puffin Books ISBN 978-0-14-240430-0

Manufactured in China